Holocaust Stories

Holocaust Stories

Aldivan Torres

Canary Of Joy

Contents

1

"Holocaust Stories"
Aldivan Torres
Holocaust Stories

By: Aldivan Torres
© 2020- Aldivan Torres
All rights reserved.
This book, including all its parts, is protected by Copyright and may not be reproduced without the permission of the author, resold or transferred.

Aldivan Torres, born in Brazil, is a consolidated writer in several genres. So far, the titles have been published in dozens of languages. From a young age, he has always been a lover of the art of writing, having consolidated a professional career from the second semester of 2013. He hopes, with his writings, to contribute to international culture, awakening the pleasure of reading in those who do not have the habit. Its mission is to win the hearts of each of its readers. In addition to literature, his main diversions are music, travel, friends, family, and the pleasure of life itself. "For literature, equality, fraternity, justice, dignity, and honor of the human being always" is his motto.

Dedication and Acknowledgments

I dedicate this work to my mother, my family, my readers, my followers, and admirers. I would be nothing without you. I especially dedicate this work to everyone who has suffered the horrors of the Holocaust.

I thank God in the first place, my relatives and myself for always believing in my potential. I will go further still.

The author

"In his heart, man plans his way, but the Lord determines his steps."

Proverbs 16: 9

Chapter 1

Chapter 2- Studying on the balcony

Chapter 3- Girlfriend's house

Chapter 4- At the Theater

Chapter 5- Sleeping room with wife

Chapter 6

Chapter 7

Chapter 8- Night in the Countryside

Chapter 9- Two years later-city

Chapter 10- Conversation- bar

Chapter 11- At home- living room

Chapter 12- Death announcement room

Chapter 13-First day of work-clothing store

Chapter 14-Gay Encounter

Chapter 15- Farewell-house of love

Chapter 16- room

Chapter 17- room

Chapter 18- Hospital

Chapter 19-Living Room-At Home

Chapter 20-Night

Final reflections on the Holocaust

Chapter 1

Father and son are in the meditation room talking about important things.

Romeo

Dad, I wanted to study. Can I start now?

Everton

Of course, Son. I will provide you with all the necessary study. I will hire a language and grammar teacher.

Romeo

Thanks Dad. I do not know how to thank you.

Everton

It was nothing. You are my only child and I have to take care of you.

Romeo

What languages will I learn?

Everton

Hebrew, English, and Spanish. I think this is extremely necessary.

Romeo

Very cool. I'm really excited.

Everton

Good, son. I like to see it like this.

Romeo

Dad, I never saw Mom again. Where did she go?

Everton

She abandoned us. He was afraid of Nazi terrorism and moved to another country.

Romeo

I'm not mad at Mom. I'm glad she was saved. What about us?

Everton

Let's face it together, son. I promise we will survive. Let's have faith in God.

Romeo

Okay, dad. I have every faith.

Chapter 2- Studying on the balcony

Teacher

Very well, Romeo. You are a very diligent student. What career do you intend to pursue?

Romeo

I want to become a doctor. I want to heal all the sick and wounded of my people. I want to save the lives of my community that is being decimated.

Teacher

Very well. It is a very honorable profession. But how are you going to study? You have no resources here and the world is at war.

Romeo

I don't know how it will happen. But one day I intend to make my dream come true.

Teacher

Will take. If you need me, I am at your disposal.

Romeo

Thank you very much!

Chapter 3- Girlfriend's house

Romeo

Kate, would you like to go to the theater with me?

Kate

But isn't it dangerous? The Romanians have invaded Russia and are bombing the city.

Romeo

Do not worry. I will protect you.

Kate

If so, then I accept your proposal.

Chapter 4- At the Theater

Kate

What a beautiful staged story. I really like going to the theater. The staging's transport us to an imaginary, just and human world. Why can't the world be like this, my love? Why is there only wars and destruction?

Romeo

People are selfish, prejudiced, individualistic, and thirsty for power. This causes significant disagreements. When an agreement cannot be reached, then the war breaks out.

Kate

Understand. Thankfully, there is only love between us. I want you forever.

Romeo

Me either. I hope the war is over soon. I have plans for our future.

Kate

I'm in the crowd, my love.

Chapter 5- Sleeping room with wife

Everton

Wake up, son. We need to escape. The war has come!

Romeo

Oh, my! What a terrible thing! It arrived very fast! What do you say, love?

Kate

I will prepare the bags. Let's go as soon as possible.

Everton

Very well, my children. You act with reason.

Chapter 6

Opponent

They wanted to run away from us! How much arrogance! Worms like you are not smart. They only serve to die!

Kate

My lord, mercy! Don't you see that we are all human beings?

Opponent

You Jews are blasphemy. We have express orders to kill them! Let's do this little by little. Your death will be slow as you deserve.

Chapter 7

Romeo

Kate, take advantage of the soldiers asleep and go get us some food.

Kate

I'll be right there, my love.

Evandro

Very well, Son! We need to survive!

Chapter 8- Night in the Countryside

Kate

I brought all the necessary food. We will eat and save for the entire trip.

Romeo

Brilliant idea. You think of everything, my love.

Evandro

I appreciate your brilliant idea, son! We are saved!

Chapter 9- Two years later-city

Evandro

We have been suffering for two years, and we are surviving. God is with us!

Romeo

Our family is a warrior. We don't give in to any situation. I am proud of you all.

Kate

We're fine thanks to the food I get.

Romeo

Truth, love. You are very convincing when you go begging. I thank you very much.

Kate

No need to thank. I do it very willingly. What will become of us and the war?

Romeo

We do not know yet. But from the speculations that we heard, there is good progress. I just feel sorry for all the people who are dying.

Kate

I also feel very sorry. They fall from weakness. You have no right to anything.

Evandro

Nazis are sentient beings. They want to kill us slowly. I'm glad you help us, Kate.

Kate

First is God. He did not allow typhus to hit us. That's why we're alive.

Evandro

Truth. First is our God. We will pray for the end of the war.

Kate

I do this every day in the company of my husband.

Romeo

True, my father. Our prayer is strong and is helping us.

Evandro

That's good. Keep doing this. It will be our salvation.

Chapter 10- Conversation- bar

Kate

I appreciate yesterday's deliverance. I was almost raped by the Germans!

Romeo

I would never allow that, my love. That's why we hide you in a safe place. No man touches my wife.

Evandro

Did you hear the news? The Russians invaded Ukraine and the Romanians were expelled. I think it is the end of our suffering.

Kate

Wonderful! God is faithful in pain and love.

Soldier

Are you Jews or Russians?

Evandro

We are Jews exiled by Nazism. Any good news?

Soldier

You can go home. The Russians defeated the Germans.

Evandro

It's ok. Let's go right now.

Chapter 11- At home- living room

Romeo

Now that it's all over, I can reveal my plans to you. How about we live in Brazil? They say it is a developing land. Are you willing to go with me?

Kate

I loved the news. I will be with you wherever you go. It is the wife's obligation.

Romeo

That's why I love you, Woman.

Evandro

To which city? Rio de Janeiro?

Romeo

You got it right. My uncle lives there and will help us adapt. It will only be happiness!

Evandro

I hope so, son!

Kate

This is the end of that massacre and the beginning of a new story. The holocaust will always be kept in our memories, but it can no longer hinder us. I want to be happy and have my children and grandchildren.

Romeo

I also want to have children with you. Our love survived the war and will last for eternity.

Kate

So be it! Long live love!

Evandro

Like the peace!

Romeo

Long live freedom!

Chapter 12- Death announcement room

Mom

My son, I just received terrible news. Her father suffered an accident at work and passed away.

Son

My God! Unbelievable. What will become of us, Mom?

Mother

We need to work, son. There is no other way out.

Son

Okay, mom. What hurts me about all this is not having revealed my sexuality to my father. I think he had a right to know.

Mother

You are silly. Of course, he knew. Everyone perceives their sexuality in their own way. What he didn't want was to get into conflict with you because he loved you so much.

Son

Truth. He was even good at that. He always respected my choices. He will miss you and I will preserve your memory forever.

Mother

You do very well, son. Now let's take care of the wake's obligations. He has to have a decent burial.

Son

It's the least we can do, Mom.

Burial

Son

This is my father's farewell. An honest, hardworking and helpful man with his family. At that moment of pain, I wanted to thank you for all the moments shared by your side. These were moments that marked my life until today. For my part, I will continue my life with faith in happy days and I promise to take your memories wherever I go. Thank you very much, my father, for everything!

Mom

Now that you are an angel of God, I ask for your protection and prayer. Bless us all on this journey on earth. We need your guidance in all problems. For our part, we will not forget his charismatic and kind figure. We will keep the values and ethics we have learned from you. We will remain united pursuing our goals. With a deep pain in the soul, we will survive. See you later!

Chapter 13-First day of work-clothing store

Son Rick

Good Morning. My name is Rick and I came to fulfill my first day at work.

Denis

Welcome, Rick. My name is Denis, and I am the owner of the store. Before I start, I'm going to give you some instructions. His role is that of a salesperson. So be the most affectionate, friendly and helpful to customers. We must always be patient with the most excited consumers. Remember that the reason is always the customers. In addition, maintaining a good reputation is essential for business. This means conquering new markets and consequently maintaining your job.

Son Rick

I understood everything. I promise to strive to fulfill my duties. That depends on my survival.

Denis

You are intelligent. Make yourself comfortable and win new customers for our company.

Son

Certainly! You can leave it to me!

Client

Good Morning! Are you the store's new salesperson?

Son

Yes. It's my first day on the job.

Client

Excellent! I am an old customer of the store. At least once a month I come to check the news.

Son

All very well. What do you want today?

Client

I want to see shirts and pants.

Son

Everything is fine. Make yourself comfortable.

Client

You have a different way. You are gay?

Son

Yes, I am, and you?

Client

I'm gay too. How about we talk later?

Son

Why not now? We are alone.

Client

You're right. Do you have a boyfriend?

Son

I'm single and you?

Client

I'm also single. What a coincidence!

Son

It seems that destiny wants to unite us. Furthermore, really liked you.

Client

Did you know that I even forgot my clothes? You are really spectacular.

Son

Nice to meet you. I needed a motivation in my life after my father's death.

Client

My feelings! Glad that our meeting brought something positive. Well, now let's take care of business.

Chapter 14-Gay Encounter

Client

The Nazis have risen to power and are pursuing our cause. What to expect from now?

Son

Dark times, my love. We live in a fundamentally different situation than when we got married. Before, we had full freedom of expression. Now, we are afraid of our shadow.

Friend

I agree with you. Everything that happens in our country is sorrowful for our community. Bad people are denouncing homosexuals who are being arrested and harassed. The government's aim is to destroy minorities. I fear for your love. It is such a true and beautiful feeling.

Son

I am also petrified. But what can we do? If we get caught, we will resist. There is no other way out.

Client

You are absolutely right, love. We must not fear death. The important thing is to live at the moment and preserve this love for posterity. It was the best thing that happened in my life, and I am sure it will be eternal.

Friend

I admire your strength. If you need my help, I'm available.

Son

Thank you very much for your support, friend.

Chapter 15- Farewell-house of love

Client

My love, I have terrible news. I have just been called up for military service.

Son

It's not possible. What will become of us now?

Client

I do not know. The future is uncertain. The reality now is that we are going to separate. I'm already packed. Have something to say?

Son

Have. I would like to say that you were the most beautiful thing that happened in my life. You appeared in a critical moment of pain and gave me hope. I can only thank the moments lived.

Client

You are also critical to me. I was discredited by love, and you made me resurface. As I told you, our love is eternal. It will not be a war that will change that.

Son

Good luck, buddy! Thank you for everything!

Prison

Police

Mr. Rick, I am the official of the Nazi government. After extensive investigations, I am arresting you for the homosexuality charge. Please join me, please.

Son

Okay, officer. I am at the disposal of the authorities. I have a clear conscience that I have not committed any crime. Being homosexual is no demerit.

Police

I only follow orders from the regime. We will not waste time discussing this. Just come with me.

Son

It's ok.

Precinct

Delegate

Good morning, Mr. Rick. Do you mean you are a homosexual? Do you confirm the report?

Rick

I don't know why you ask me if they've investigated my whole life. Yes, I am a very proud homosexual.

Precinct

Very well. Then I will read your sentence. You are sentenced to six months in prison for violating the terms of paragraph 175.

Rick

Everything is fine. I am ready for martyrdom.

Release

Today was my release. I spent two years being tortured in this prison and my memories are terrible. Among the atrocities committed, I had to participate in medical experiments trying to reverse my sexual orientation, electroshock, I was beaten and sexually assaulted. What I have suffered here I do not wish for my worst enemy. But I survived, and I thank God for that. I am going to start my life over now completely broken. I lost my companion to the war, and I am being expelled from my country. My countrymen hate me for being a homosexual, which is not my fault. I consider myself a phoenix for having survived this whole process. I will now go on with my life with faith in God in the hope of being happy again. The only certainty I have is that I will never stop being what I am because that is part of my identity. I am not a coward.

Chapter 16- room

Father

I have bad news. Nazi Germany annexed Austria to its territory. This can be considered the beginning of the holocaust for us. According to a published decree, they will persecute Jews, homosexuals and us Gypsies, among other minorities. The police are already investigating our caste. This is the prelude to the end.

Daughter

My God. What will become of us? We are peaceful people. We cannot be exterminated by these madmen.

Mother

Let's have faith in Santa Sara. She will protect us. These demons are not going to triumph over us. We will survive.

Daughter

Good to have faith, my mother. Father, what's going on with our clan?

Father

They are chasing our moral laws. They are meddling in marriage issues, they excluded our children from school, they use the strength of the army to frighten us, and they are charging high taxes. Many Roma is being deported to concentration camps where they are suffering the worst types of torture. Times are bleak.

Daughter

How horrible.

Mother

How long will it be, my love? This is going to become unbearable.

Father

I don't know, woman. Let us wait for the next events.

Terrace

Daughter

Dad, why are we hated? What harm have we done to the world?

Father

No harm has been done, daughter. We are a humble and struggling people. It is our bad opponents. They feel like the pure race on the planet.

Daughter

They are really cowards. But, changing the subject, could you tell me a little about the history of our people?

Father

With pleasure, daughter. Our people are from Northwest India. Due to internal differences, we were forced to emigrate towards the West from the sixth century onwards. From then on, we went through intense deprivation. We were slaves, humiliated and persecuted for our beliefs. Then we spread to various points on the planet. We reach all of Europe, the Middle East and North Africa. In the 19th century, there was the third migratory phenomenon, and we reached the Americas. Today we are a world clan.

Daughter

What a beautiful story. I am proud to be a gypsy. I know it is a difficult time, but I think it will be okay.

Father

Children's faith. Yes, everything will be fine. I promise.

Daughter

Thanks Dad. I'm happy to be your daughter.

Father

And I am happy to be your father. Remember, my little one, whatever happens, I will always be with you.

Daughter

I believe. Promise is debt.

Father

I will have to leave. Go home to be with your mother.

Daughter

It's ok. Take care, father. Enemies are everywhere.

Father

Do not worry. I will be fine.

Chapter 17- room

Messenger

I came to give you some terrible news. Ignatius was arrested by the Nazi soldiers. Now it's praying that he can get out of this. Most prisoners die in the concentration camp itself.

Mom

I can't believe that my only love was arrested by those despots. What will become of our family? Ignacio is an example of a father, companion and honest man. In our entire clan he is praised. He is a leader both inside and outside the home. Without it, we are totally aimless.

Messenger

I understand your distress, madam. But there is nothing to be done at this point. What I recommend is to be cautious with these powerful enemies. They are capable of anything. They are capable of killing and torturing human beings without any qualms.

Mother

I know that. Thank you for the advice. I will take care of myself and my daughter. We will be very cautious. I promise we will survive.

Messenger

That's the way it is spoken, madam. Be well, little one.

Daughter

Thank you, sir. Be well too.

Living room

Messenger

Another bad news came. Ignacio just passed away. My condolences!

Mom

My God! What a tragedy! We were already hoping for something like that. Gypsies are being wiped out by this fascist regime.

Daughter

My only father! Poor thing! What are we going to do now, Mom?

Mom

We will face our destiny, daughter. If these monsters want us, they will have it. If necessary, we will die as martyrs.

Daughter

I'm petrified, mom!

Mom

Calm down, daughter! Then to depend on me, you are saved! Thank you, boy. You were of great help in giving us this news. Go in peace!

Messenger

Thank you, Madam! Be at peace too.

Square

Soldier

Your turn has come! A decree was issued to bring all Roma together. We will take you to the concentration camp at Auschwitz.

Mom

We are ready! You can take us!

Daughter

We go with you, but our God does not sleep. Justice will be served.

Soldier

Stop dreaming, little fool. You are in our hands.

Departure from the camp

Daughter

Mom, we're free. We survive! I can't believe it!

Mother

Thank goodness, daughter. We were raped morally all the time, but we resisted. Thanks to Saint Sara we were released. The good will always overcome evil. Too bad my love was not so lucky. They are sequels of war that will remain in our minds forever.

Daughter

Mom, will we be happy after everything we've been through?

Mother

I don't know, daughter. But do we have another choice? We need to move forward with our heads held high. We need to find a reason to live and survive. Maktub! So, it was written.

Daughter

Great sage. I love you mom. Always stay with me.

Mother

I promise I will never abandon you. Together or separately, we will always be soul mates.

Chapter 18- Hospital

Doctor

Dear lady, I have some bad news. Despite our best efforts, her husband has just died of acute pneumonia. I am so sorry!

Women

My God! It cannot be! Damn disease! What will I do now? I have a young daughter to look after. Really, I have no way out.

Doctor

Calm down, lady! I'm sure your husband would not be happy with your discouragement. He wants you to follow your life with your head held high. Think that life is beautiful and full of surprises. May only happiness come to you.

Daughter

He's right, Mom. We will survive together. Whatever the challenge, we will surely overcome it. I'm going to help you. Let us trust in God!

Mother

Thank you for the words. What pride of this little warrior! I promise I will fight for us. Let's move on!

Daughter

That's how you talk, mom!

Chapter 19-Living Room-At Home

Neighbor

Friend, do you know the latest news?

Mom

I'm not. Could you tell me?

Neighbor

Of course, yes. It will be a pleasure. Adolf Hitler's troops invaded the country. We are completely dominated. As an obligation of the regime, we have to use our belief symbols so that we can be identified. They hate us and want to exterminate us, friend. I'm petrified.

Mom

My God! What a terror! Damn Nazis! Because of their prejudice they are leading us to a world war! But we have to resist.

Daughter

What is happening to our people?

Neighbor

We are being chased, beaten and humiliated. We are treated as if we were animals. Times are bleak.

Mom

Do you have any more information to give us?

Neighbor

Yes. Be cautious. Do not trust anyone. At all times, Nazi officers are ambushing to arrest and kill our youth. They are monsters searching for blood. They are the plague of the apocalypse.

Mom

I suppose! Leave it, we will be cautious.

Neighbor

I'm cool with that, friend. Now I have to leave. Stay in peace!

Mom

Go with God!

Daughter

Thanks for everything. This helped us a lot.

Room

Mom

Good night daughter! The postman delivered a summons. The government is ordering us to work in the industry. From each Jewish family, they are choosing two people. We are the chosen ones.

Daughter

I will work? I'm just a child!

Mom

Do not worry. Children don't work. They only accompany their parents. I will make sure of that myself.

Daughter

What a relief! And what will happen to our cousins and aunts?

Mom

I do not know. But I suppose they will be wiped out! This is part of the Nazi plan. They want to destroy us little by little.

Daughter

My God! How much cruelty in this world! Let the meteor come and destroy these bastards.

Mom

If the meteor came, it would destroy us all. Therefore, God does not give this permission.

Daughter

You're right! God is always good! God is faithful in love and pain. All honor and glory to him forever!

Mom

Yes. He is the only one who never leaves us. Let's have faith that we will survive!

Daughter

So be it!

Chapter 20-Night

Mom

Today is another day of human firing. Who of us will die?

Daughter

Calm down, Mom. There are still many men in the camp. We still have a long time to survive.

Mom

And do you speak with all that calm? Any life is important. Each human being carries dreams and a story. These monsters have no right to destroy dreams. They are not God!

Daughter

I agree! But in the aspect of survival, it relieves us. Being a woman is an advantage at this point. This allows us to dream.

Mom

Yes, true. What are your dreams, daughter?

Daughter

I want to graduate in law so that I can defend the rights of the minority. The war taught me to side with the most humble, marginalized and persecuted. I want to be their guardian angel.

Mom

Your attitude is commendable. I am proud to be your mother.

Daughter

And I am proud to be your daughter. It's going to be okay, Mom. Believe it!

Mother

I admire your strength and hope. Yes, I believe that we will win. Let's go to sleep!

Daughter

Sweet Dreams. God bless us.

Field

Soldier

Work, slave! I want to have the pleasure of watching your sweat drip down! Come on, work!

Mother

Have pity, sir! I'm just a woman.

Daughter

That. Have pity on my mother!

Soldier

Why would I have mercy? What justice is there in this world? I only know the law of the strongest.

Mother

Don't you fear God?

Soldier

I fear! But honestly speaking, I'm just an order-taker!

Mother

I understand. May God have mercy on your soul.

Soldier

Thank you very much, Madam! You can rest now. God heard you!

Daughter

God bless you!

Field

Daughter

We're free, Mom! I did not say? We are victorious.

Mother

Yes. We are big winners! When we think we are unharmed, it is a cause for celebration. Many died in gas chambers, tortured and humiliated. There were also murders, bomb explosions and horror show. Although we survived, we will never forget all the tragedies. This will stay in our memory forever.

Daughter

Yes, mom. We will always remember. But the important thing now is that we are free. We will not give up being happy for the rest of our lives. Let's build a new story. Let's do this for my father.

Mother

Okay, I promise. We will rebuild our lives remembering my husband.

Daughter

That's how you talk!

Mother

Our love is infinite! Together forever!

Daughter

For sure, with God first!

At home

Daughter

Dad, I love you. With the war approaching, I can clearly see how good you were with all my family. With his work, he gives us everything we need. With his affection and values, he strokes us. I am grateful for everything she did with us and for being this young warrior and full of dreams.

Father

Thank you, daughter. But I have done nothing but my obligation. You and your mother are the most important people in my life. With the war imminent and the holocaust against our people, I cannot promise anymore. But you can be sure that I would give my life for you.

Daughter

I know that, father. I don't blame you. With your support and prayers, I'm sure we'll survive. The good will always overcome evil.

Father

I believe that too, daughter.

Wife

I also have to thank you. I appreciate your companionship, your financial assistance and your love. I remember that fateful encounter at a costume ball on Halloween. You were the most elegant wizard at the party, so I fell in love instantly. My biggest emotion was when you asked me to dance. There was my chance to win you over. I swear I didn't do it out of interest. Despite being in the presence of a successful entrepreneur, I saw beyond that. I saw a kind, honest and caring man. Even if you were poor, you were my achievement. That's how we got close, and we're still together today.

Father

I remember that day well. You were the first woman who caught my attention. Calling for a contradiction was a way of getting closer. But I always wanted you because you were different. His sense of simplicity and humility won me over. I do not regret my choice because I am happy in this marriage until now. I love you!

Wife

Love you too. Living that feeling was what liberated me from a monotonous life. The war is approaching, but I am not afraid. Our love is untouchable.

Father

Yes, definitely. You and my daughter are my untouchable loves.

Wife

I have a request to make. Before they catch us, how about we go on a trip?

Father

Good idea. What place suggests us to travel?

Wife

Which place do you like best, daughter?

Daughter

I want to go to the beach. I love to see the little fish jumping around.

Father

Very well. I loved the suggestion. Let's spend a day at the beach and enjoy our provisional freedom.

Beach

Daughter

Look at all this nature and the freedom it gives us. Why aren't men simple? Why are there races that are superior to others? Aren't we all the same before God?

Father

This is called prejudice. It is one of the evils that the human being carries in the soul. Let us not follow this example. Let us live what Christ has taught us. "We cannot change the world, but we can change ourselves".

Daughter

True, father. I will always live according to my ethics. I will continue to be honest, hardworking and respecting minorities.

Father

That's right, daughter! You are my pride.

Daughter

Thanks, Dad!

Mom

You are examples, my loves. Before us is a compelling enemy. Nazism preaches a pure race and hatred for minorities. They want to destroy us. I don't know how to escape it, but it will come to an end. Jews are also human.

Father

That's right, woman! They are not going to destroy us completely. We are God's chosen people. We are suffering this trial because of our ancestors' mistakes. Prophecies are fulfilled. But everything will be fine, you can be sure!

Mom

Thank goodness, love! Let's face it together!

Daughter

We are already winners, Mom. Now let's forget about the problems and enjoy this wonderful beach.

Mom

You're right. Let's enjoy this good time.

At home

Soldier

I came to give a warning. Things are getting complicated for Jews. So, get out of here while there's time.

Father

I am not a man to run away from problems. We are ready to face our destiny. We are no better than our brothers. So, we will be.

Soldier

This is crazy. Don't you think about your family? His wife so beautiful and his daughter so full of life. Know that the Nazis are unforgiving to everyone!

Father

I always think about my family. But this decision is theirs too. We will not leave our home. We are not going to abandon our story because of fear.

Mother

You have all my support, love. Cowardice is a dishonor to warriors. If we have to die, we will die with honor.

Daughter

Exactly, Mom. We are ready to fight!

Soldier

Well, you know who. Then don't say I didn't warn you.

Road

Soldier

Are you Jews?

Father

Yes, we are.

Soldier

Your arrest warrant has arrived. We will take you to the concentration camp.

Father

We are ready!

Mom

We expected this already. You can take us.

Daughter

Let's go with you.

Train

Daughter

Where are we going, Mother?

Mother

To Poland, daughter. It is there that we will suffer the horrors of the Holocaust.

Daughter

Let us be strong! Everything is as God wants!

Soldier

I disagree! In that case, that's how Hitler wants it.

Father

Your master would not have this authority if God did not allow it. Remember that one day it is the hunt and the other day it is the hunter.

Soldier

You are not in a position to threaten. Be quiet that we are already arriving.

Father

It's ok! Do not get angry.

Concentration camp

Daughter

You saved me! Why did it?

Soldier

Because it had to be that way. It was written in your story.

Daughter

My story is destroyed! You don't know the pain I'm feeling. I lost my parents in the concentration camp. They were my lifelong companions. They had so much hope of surviving. However, now it's all over.

Soldier

You can resume your story. You are a young woman, and you have a life ahead of you. Forget what happened in the war. It is the only chance you have to be happy.

Daughter

I know that. I will take your advice, guardian angel. Thank you for everything!

Soldier

No need to thank! Your faith saved you.

Final reflections on the Holocaust

Journalist

What was the Holocaust?

Divine

The holocaust was the genocide of Jews and several minorities across the Nazi state. The holocaust occurred in all territories occupied by Germany during World War II. About two-thirds of the Jewish population residing in Europe have been wiped out. Among them, more than one million children, two million women and three million men. In addition, Gypsies, Poles, Communists, homosexuals, Soviet prisoners of war, Jehovah's Witnesses and the disabled also died. In total, more than eleven million people were killed. With a network of more than forty thousand facilities, the Nazis focused on their goal of exterminating, torturing and exploiting the victims. In concentration camps, victims were subjected to slave labor until they died. Shots and instruments of torture, such as gas chambers, were also common. The Third Reich was known as the genocidal state.

Journalist

How did it all start?

Divine

From the second half of the 19th century, this process of ethnic exclusion began with the ideas of some German thinkers who preached racism. Jews were seen as an enemy race. This prejudice grew more and more, and they concluded that the extermination of the Jewish race was necessary.

Journalist

How terrible. I conclude that Nazism was the worst thing that happened in the world. What is your opinion, Divine?

Divine

It was a disastrous thing. The Lord Jesus loves life and those responsible for this project really did not get forgiveness. Human blood is sacred. I will teach you what I learned from my father. We must love, forgive, share and evolve. We need to be real humans. Only then will we get to heaven. Understood. Say goodbye to this job by singing a song.

Divine

It will be an honor.

Divine sings the song of his story. A sense of peace fills the room. There was much more to talk about the Holocaust, this dark period in our history. But the past should only serve as a reflection for good times of evolution to come to humanity.

Final

www.ingramcontent.com/pod-product-compliance
Lightning Source LLC
LaVergne TN
LVHW021050100526
838202LV00082B/5421